Cat Nap

First published in 2008
by Wayland

This paperback edition published in 2009

Text copyright © Claire Llewellyn 2008
Illustration copyright © Jacqueline East 2008

Wayland
338 Euston Road
London NW1 3BH

Wayland Australia
Hachette Children's Books
Level 17/207 Kent Street
Sydney, NSW 2000

The rights of Claire Llewellyn to be identified as the Author and
Jacqueline East to be identified as the Illustrator of this Work have been
asserted by them in accordance with the Copyright,
Designs and Patents Act, 1988.

Series editor: Louise John
Cover design: Paul Cherrill
Design: D.R.ink
Consultant: Shirley Bickler

A CIP catalogue record for this book is available from the British Library.

ISBN 9780750251754 (hbk)
ISBN 9780750251761 (pbk)

Printed in China

Wayland is a division of Hachette Children's Books,
an Hachette Livre UK Company

Cat Nap

Written by Claire Llewellyn
Illustrated by Jacqueline East

WAYLAND

Coco the cat wanted a nap.
She curled up in
the cupboard.

5

Mum opened the door.
"Meow!" said Coco and
she jumped out.

Coco curled up on the bed.
Along came baby Ella.
"Waaaahhh!" she cried.

Coco went downstairs.

Dad was downstairs.
"Shoo, Coco!" he said.
"Get off my chair."

Coco went into the garden.

But Digby was in
the garden.

12

He ran after Coco.

Coco curled up
on a chair, but there
were birds in the garden.

"Tweet, tweet!" said
the birds.

Along came Pip.

"Hello, Coco," he
said. "Let's play ball!"

But Coco didn't want
to play. She wanted a nap.

Coco curled up under
a bush. Along came a bee.

"Buzz, buzz!" said the bee.

"Meow!" said Coco.

At last it was quiet.

Coco curled up in the tree
and went to sleep.

Then down came the rain!

START READING is a series of highly enjoyable books for beginner readers. They have been carefully graded to match the Book Bands widely used in schools. This enables readers to be sure they choose books that match their own reading ability.

The Bands are:

Pink / Band 1

Red / Band 2

Yellow / Band 3

Blue / Band 4

Green / Band 5

Orange / Band 6

Turquoise / Band 7

Purple / Band 8

Gold / Band 9

START READING books can be read independently or shared with an adult. They promote the enjoyment of reading through satisfying stories supported by fun illustrations.

Claire Llewellyn has written many books for children. Some of them are about real things like animals or the Moon. Others are storybooks, like this one. Claire has two children of her own, but they are getting too big for stories like this. She hopes that you will enjoy reading her stories instead now!

Jacqueline East scratched her first drawing into her mum's sideboard when she was six! She has enjoyed drawing animals ever since and has a naughty dog called Scampi, who often appears in her books! When Jacqueline is not drawing, she likes to dance and play the guitar.